WYNKEN, BLYNKEN
AND NOD

Wynken, Blynken and Nod

By Eugene Field

Illustrated by Barbara Cooney

HASTINGS HOUSE, *Book Publishers*
Mamaroneck, NY

WYNKEN, BLYNKEN
AND NOD

Wynken, Blynken, and Nod one night
   Sailed off in a wooden shoe—
Sailed on a river of crystal light,
   Into a sea of dew.

"Where are you going, and what do you wish?"
　　The old moon asked the three.
"We have come to fish for the herring fish
　　That live in this beautiful sea;
　　Nets of silver and gold have we!"
　　　　Said Wynken,
　　　　Blynken,
　　　　And Nod.

The old moon laughed and sang a song,
    As they rocked in the wooden shoe,
And the wind that sped them all night long
    Ruffled the waves of dew.

The little stars were the herring fish
   That lived in that beautiful sea—
"Now cast your nets wherever you wish—
   Never afeard are we";
So cried the stars to the fishermen three:
      Wynken,
      Blynken,
      And Nod.

All night long their nets they threw
    To the stars in the twinkling foam —
Then down from the skies came the wooden shoe,
    Bringing the fishermen home;

'Twas all so pretty a sail it seemed
   As if it could not be,
And some folks thought 'twas a dream they'd dreamed
   Of sailing that beautiful sea—
But I shall name you the fishermen three:
   Wynken,
   Blynken,
   And Nod.

Wynken and Blynken are two little eyes,
  And Nod is a little head,
And the wooden shoe that sailed the skies
  Is a wee one's trundle-bed.

So shut your eyes while mother sings
   Of wonderful sights that be,
And you shall see the beautiful things
   As you rock in the misty sea,
   Where the old shoe rocked the fishermen three:
      Wynken,
      Blynken,
      And Nod.

EUGENE FIELD, American poet and journalist, was born in St. Louis on September 3, 1850, and died in 1895. Two of his poems are now a part of the permanent treasury of poems for children. These are "Little Boy Blue" and "Wynken, Blynken and Nod," the latter of which is reprinted from *Poems of Childhood,* by the kind permission of Charles Scribner's Sons.

BARBARA COONEY was born in Brooklyn, New York. She is a graduate of Smith College. She has illustrated over eighty books for major publishers and it was for *Chanticleer and the Fox* (T. Y. Crowell Co.), that she was awarded her first Caldecott Medal in 1959. She won a second Caldecott in 1980 for *The Ox-Cart Man* (Viking). In private life, the artist is Mrs. Charles Talbot Porter and makes her home in Pepperell, Massachusetts.